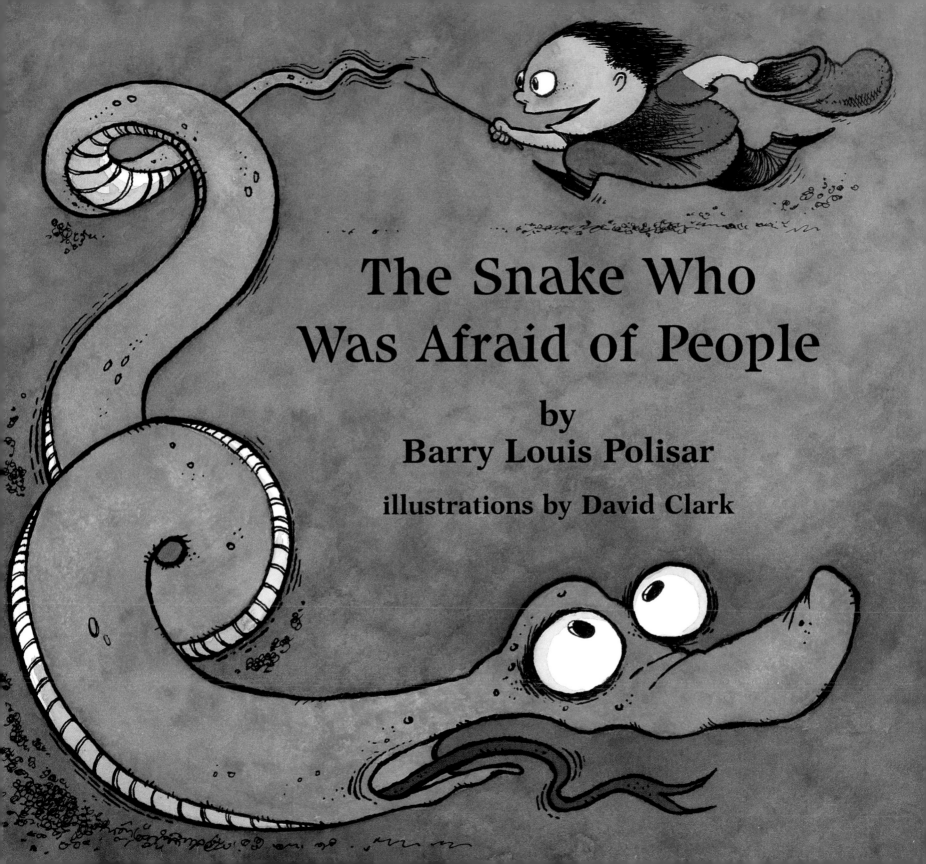

The Snake Who
Was Afraid of People

by
Barry Louis Polisar

illustrations by David Clark

Leo was a normal snake. He liked to sun himself on the rocks, and he liked to hide in the shade of a wood pile on real hot days.

But unlike other snakes, who would occasionally wriggle up onto people's porches to show how brave they were, Leo was absolutely, positively *afraid* of people.

The other snakes would tease Leo for being afraid, but he didn't care. He *was* afraid. He'd seen people before and he didn't like them.

Sometimes Leo would be lying peacefully under a pile of leaves when all of a sudden someone would be standing over him, poking him with a long stick.

If he were lucky, he could scare the person away by coiling up and sticking out his tongue. But usually, he wasn't lucky. Usually, it would be Leo who had to run away as the person continued to jab at him with a stick. Once, some older men even shot at him with a gun.

Leo didn't want anything to do with people.

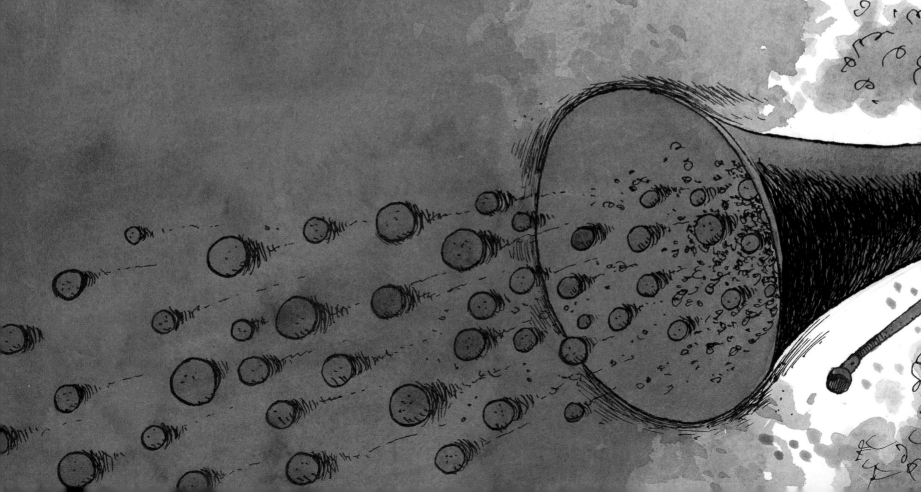

His mother would try to make him feel better by saying, "People are just as afraid of you as you are of them."

His father would say, "Most people aren't really dangerous and won't hurt you."

But their advice never made Leo feel any better.

One day Leo was playing with his friend Lazlo by the rocks in the pond near his home.

All of a sudden a man appeared out of nowhere. Before they could escape, the man bent over and grabbed Lazlo.

Leo watched in horror as Lazlo was taken away.

Leo stayed closer to home after that, but one spring morning while he was playing near the wood pile behind his house, he heard a noise. A little boy was walking through the woods, carrying a stick and a big brown bag. Leo quickly darted underneath an old board to hide, but it was too late. He had been spotted.

The boy swooped down and grabbed him and threw him into the sack. Leo was captured!

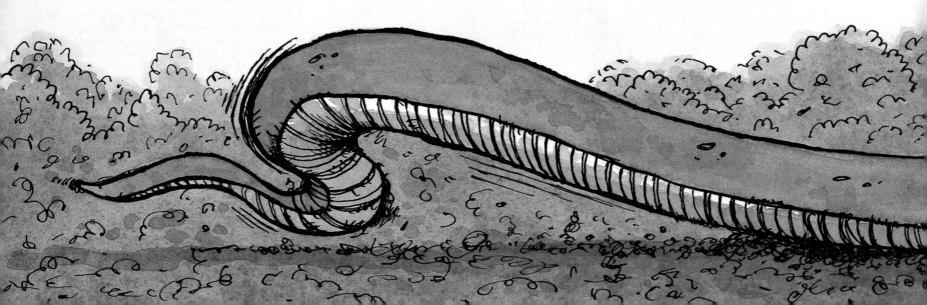

It was awful in there. It was dark and smelly and the bag made his skin itch.

After a long while, the boy took him out of the bag to show Leo to his friends. He poked him with a stick to make him move.

Leo tried to scare them by sticking out his tongue and hissing, but they weren't afraid. In fact, they just laughed at him, and then they put him in a big jar.

It was hot and stuffy inside the jar. The boy had poked a few air holes in the lid but they didn't let in too much air. To make matters worse, the boy set the jar on a window ledge in the sun. It became so hot that Leo could hardly breathe.

Leo was tired and thirsty and very lonely. He wondered if he would ever get back home to see his family and friends again.

The next day, while the boy was at school, the boy's mother took the jar down from the window sill and brought it into the bathroom.

She leaned over the toilet, dropped Leo in and flushed it! Leo felt like he was going to drown. Swimming against the swirling water, he managed to pull himself over the rim of the toilet bowl and fell to the floor wriggling and hissing. The woman stepped back and Leo squirmed out of the bathroom as fast as he could.

But where would he hide?

He wriggled into the living room and slithered underneath the sofa. Before he knew what was happening the woman began whacking at him with a broom.

He moved as fast as he could and coiled up behind the television set.

Finally the woman opened the front door and, using her broom, tried to push him toward the door.

Leo saw his chance. He darted for the door and slid across the front porch.

Just as he was slithering across the yard, the school bus let the children off at the corner.

They all saw him and a dozen kids began running after him, shouting and screaming. A dog was chasing him, too.

Just when it seemed that Leo would be captured or trampled to death, he heard a familiar hiss.

Leo turned and saw his old friend Lazlo calling to him from a hole beneath a tree. Could it possibly be? He wriggled over and slid down the hole.

Once inside the safety of the hole, Lazlo embraced Leo and introduced him to his friends. It seemed that each of them had been a prisoner and each had managed to escape just like Leo. Now they spent their days roaming the neighborhood trying to help other snakes who were in trouble.

Lazlo had been rescued by a group of snakes who operated an underground railroad that re-united snakes with their families. Each night one of the rescued snakes would leave for the journey back home.

Lazlo invited Leo to stay with them until it was his turn to go. The other snakes taught Leo songs and each night they'd lie around their camp and sing.

After a week and a half it was Leo's turn to go. At midnight, under a full moon, he said goodbye to Lazlo and his new friends and headed for home.

Some of the other snakes had made Leo new clothes so no one would recognize him along the way. And his disguise worked.

After two days, Leo finally arrived back home. He was happy to see his family and friends again, and they were thrilled to see him.

He told everyone what had happened and how Lazlo had helped him escape. He was a big celebrity—even the brave snakes who used to tease Leo were impressed with his story.

No one teases Leo anymore—they understand why he is still afraid of people.

Thanks to my wife Roni,
who gave me the idea for this sequel
and to Cousin Shelby,
who helped it wriggle along.

The Snake Who Was Afraid of People
© 1987, 1988, 1993 by Barry Louis Polisar
Artwork © 1993 by David Clark

Published by Rainbow Morning Music
2121 Fairland Road, Silver Spring, MD 20904

Hardback ISBN 0-938663-16-X

A different edition of this book was
previously published in 1988